FELIX AND THE PIED PIPER

by Damian Harvey and Esther Hernando

My name is Felix, and I live in a town called Hamelin. I want to tell you about something that happened when I was a young boy.

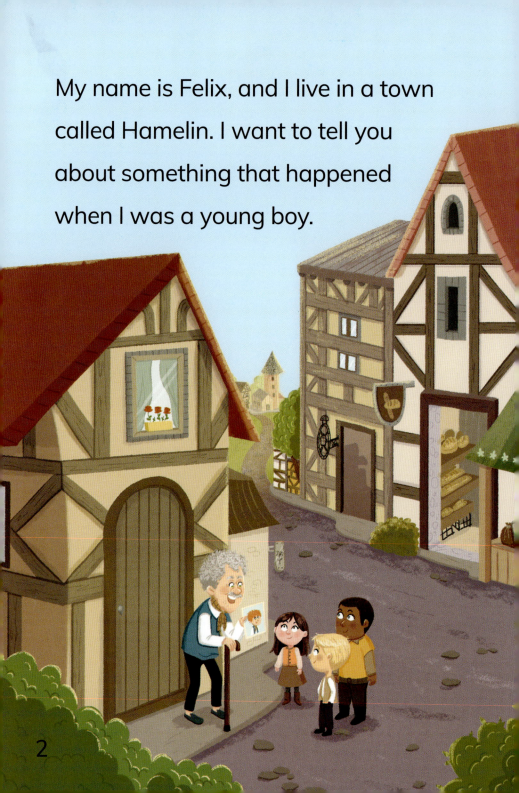

At that time, the town was full of rats.

There were rats everywhere.

They got into all the houses and they ate all the food.

One day, I saw a strange-looking man walking into town. He was dressed from head to toe in red, yellow and blue. In his hand, he held a pipe. I'd never seen anyone like him before.

4

The man walked to the mayor's house.
"I'm the Pied Piper," he said. "I can
get rid of your rats."
"Come inside," said the mayor.

When the Pied Piper came out of
the mayor's house, he looked very happy.

The Pied Piper began to play his pipe and the most amazing thing happened. Rats started running out of the houses. They ran out of doorways. They jumped out of windows. They scampered from holes in the ground.

I watched as the Pied Piper skipped along the street, playing his pipe. It was as if he had cast a magic spell on the rats.

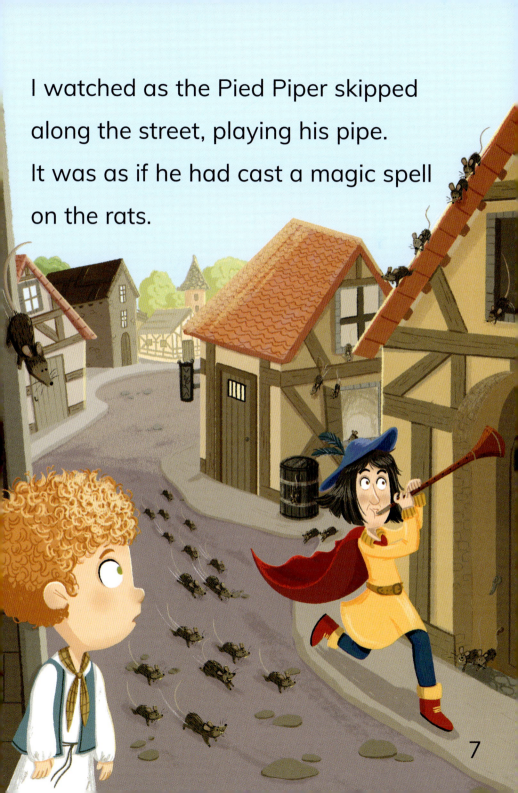

The next day, there was not a single rat to be seen. The Pied Piper came back into town. He walked down to the mayor's house and went inside.

But this time, when he came back out,
he was not happy at all.
He stomped off up the street.
"It looks like the mayor has upset him,"
said my father.

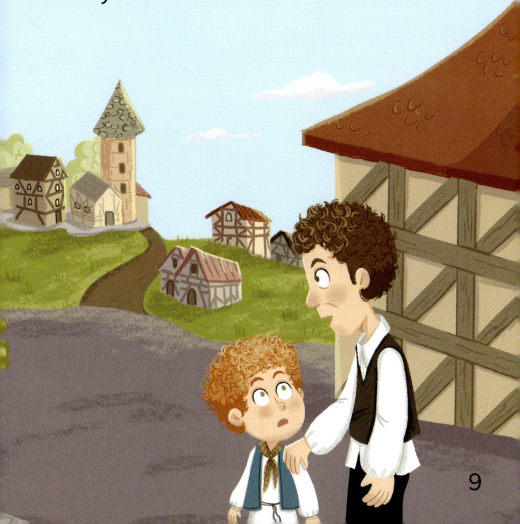

That night, I heard music.

It was the most beautiful music

I'd ever heard. It seemed to be

calling to me. I tiptoed down the stairs

and opened the front door.

The Pied Piper was playing his pipe and
skipping down the street. All the children
in Hamelin were following him.

They looked so happy.

Before I knew what was happening,
I was following too.

The next morning, I woke up in a big field. All the children from Hamelin were there, but there was no sign of the Pied Piper.

We spent the day sitting by the river and playing in the sun. It was a beautiful place, and we all felt happy.

As the day went on, some children wanted to go home. But none of us knew where we were or which way to go.

Then it started getting dark. We were all very frightened. We didn't know if we would see our homes and families ever again.

Just then, we heard the Pied Piper's beautiful music calling to us again. The music made us feel happy and we all started to follow it.

Before I knew what was happening,
I was walking back into town with
the other children.
When I got there, my mother and father
were waiting to greet me.

My father told me why the piper was angry. The mayor had not paid him for getting rid of the rats. When the children disappeared, the people begged the mayor to pay.
As soon as the Pied Piper had got his gold, he came to bring us all back home.

Since then, I've not seen a single rat in Hamelin. I've not seen the Pied Piper either. But to this day, I have never liked the sound of pipe music.

Story order

Look at these 5 pictures and captions.
Put the pictures in the right order
to retell the story.

1

The mayor did not pay the piper.

2

The children followed the piper.

3

The rats followed the piper.

4

The town was full of rats.

5

The children woke up in a field.

Independent Reading

This series is designed to provide an opportunity for your child to read on their own. These notes are written for you to help your child choose a book and to read it independently.
In school, your child's teacher will often be using reading books which have been banded to support the process of learning to read. Use the book band colour your child is reading in school to help you make a good choice. *Felix and the Pied Piper* is a good choice for children reading at Gold Band in their classroom to read independently. The aim of independent reading is to read this book with ease, so that your child enjoys the story and relates it to their own experiences.

About the book
Felix lived in Hamelin as a young boy, and he remembers when the Pied Piper came to get rid of the town's rats ...

Before reading
Help your child to learn how to make good choices by asking: "Why did you choose this book? Why do you think you will enjoy it?" Look at the cover together and ask: "What do you think the story will be about?" Support your child to think of what they already know about the story context and remind them of the story *The Pied Piper of Hamelin*. Read the title aloud and ask: "What is special about the man playing the pipe?" Remind your child that they can try to sound out the letters to make a word if they get stuck. Decide together whether your child will read the story independently or read it aloud to you.

During reading

If reading aloud, support your child if they hesitate or ask for help by telling the word. Remind your child of what they know and what they can do independently. If reading to themselves, remind your child that they can come and ask for your help if stuck.

After reading

Support comprehension by asking your child to tell you about the story. Use the story order puzzle to encourage your child to retell the story in the right sequence, in their own words. The correct sequence can be found on the next page.
Give your child a chance to respond to the story: "Did you have a favourite part? Did you expect the children to make it back home to Hamelin?"
Help your child think about the messages in the book that go beyond the story and ask: "Was the Pied Piper wrong to punish the mayor for not paying him? Was this punishment fair?"

Extending learning

Think about the story with your child, and make comparisons with the story *The Pied Piper of Hamelin*. Help your child understand the story structure by using the same story context and adding different elements. "Let's make up a new story about Felix when he follows the Pied Piper's music. Where does he go? What happens in your story?"
In the classroom, your child's teacher may be looking at fronted adverbial phrases to add information to sentences. On a few of the pages, look at some of these with your child, such as: At that time; One day; As soon as the piper had got his gold; Since then.

Franklin Watts
First published in Great Britain in 2024
by Hodder and Stoughton
Copyright © Hodder and Stoughton, Ltd

Series Editors: Jackie Hamley and Melanie Palmer
Series Advisors and Development Editors: Dr Sue Bodman and Glen Franklin
Series Designers: Cathryn Gilbert and Peter Scoulding

A CIP catalogue record for this book is
available from the British Library.

ISBN 978 1 4451 9106 5 (hbk)
ISBN 978 1 4451 9108 9 (pbk)
ISBN 978 1 4451 9107 2 (ebook)

Printed in China

Franklin Watts
An imprint of
Hachette Children's Group
Part of Hodder and Stoughton
Carmelite House
50 Victoria Embankment
London EC4Y 0DZ

An Hachette UK Company
www.hachette.co.uk

www.reading-champion.co.uk

Answer to Story order: 4, 3, 1, 2, 5